THE TRAMPLED PRIMROSE

THE TRAMPLED PRIMROSE AND OTHER STORIES

Honor Rudnitzky

The Book Guild Ltd
Sussex, England

First published in Great Britain in 2002 by
The Book Guild Ltd
25 High Street
Lewes, East Sussex
BN7 2LU

Typesetting in Baskerville by
IML Typographers, Birkenhead, Merseyside

Printed in Great Britain by
Bookcraft (Bath) Ltd, Avon

A catalogue record for this book is available from
The British Library.

ISBN 1 85776 671 7

CONTENTS

THE TRAMPLED PRIMROSE

"That's a good girl now," said Auntie Jean, "you run along and play. We don't want you tiring your poor mother."

Ellen wanted to say, "I wasn't tiring her. I was just sitting beside her," but Auntie Jean was not the sort of person you argued with. Nobody seemed to want a small child in the sick-room, or anywhere else in the house. Slowly she went down the stairs, trailing Polyanna behind her. At the bottom the doll's arm came off and she kicked it before her into the kitchen. She did not really care for that silly old doll. The back door stood open, and listlessly she sat down on the step and leant her cheek against the door. The tears were not far away.

"Well, well, what's all this?" said May, suddenly towering above her with a great basket of washing. "That's no place to leave poor Polyanna. I nearly put my foot on her. Lost an arm, has she? Well, we'll soon fix that." She set the basket on the kitchen table. "Now wait till I see. I had a crochet hook here somewhere."

Ellen wanted to show she was not interested, but in spite of herself she watched as May poked about inside the doll and expertly hooked its arm on to the elastic cord.

"There you are now. Right as rain."

She expects me to cheer up, thought Ellen.

"Thank you, May," she said with a wan little smile.

"Bless you, lovey," said May and gave her a hug. Then quite

suddenly the tears came, she could not explain why. She buried her face in May's scratchy old apron and felt her plump warm arms around her.

"Don't you be fretting now about your Mammy, lovey. She's going to get better, never you fear."

Ellen nodded, then gave a long sniff.

"Here's one of your Da's hankies," said May, pulling it out of the basket. "Blow. There, that's better." Her hands were red and smelt of soap. "Now just you sit up there on the table," she said, setting her up beside the washing. "Your Auntie brought some of these wee cakes for your Mammy's tea, and they'll never miss one. But don't you be letting on." She wagged a finger at Ellen.

Ellen smiled, feeling almost like a conspirator, and sank her teeth into one of Auntie Jean's angel cakes.

Just then they heard Auntie Jean's voice. Instantly Ellen buried the rest of the bun in the washing and brushed the tell-tale crumbs from her mouth. May whipped off her rough apron and pulled down her sleeves.

"So this is where you are," said Auntie Jean in the doorway. "You ought to be out in the sun this lovely day." She flashed a quick, but not really friendly smile. It always annoyed her that "that girl", as she called May, never wore a cap, as by Auntie Jean's standards a maid should.

Ellen's eyes followed the cakes as they went upstairs on the tray, and she hoped Auntie Jean would not notice there was one missing.

"Did they notice?" she asked when May came down.

"Notice what?"

"About the cakes."

"Bless your heart, no. And if they had, I'd have said a wee mouse got it, wouldn't I?" she winked at Ellen. "Your Auntie's always on about the mice in this old house."

Ellen ate the rest of the cake thoughtfully and considered May. She was not really like a grown-up at all. Not a bit like the maid they had before May came, always telling you not to do this or that and to wipe your feet on the mat. May was more like a big sister, a very nice big sister. And another thing – she did not seem to be in awe of Auntie Jean.

Upstairs Auntie Jean was saying, "You shouldn't let that child hang about in the kitchen so much. She's looking quite peaky. Needs to be out in the sun."

"Yes, it's difficult," said her mother and sighed. "Perhaps we could ask May to take her out sometimes."

"You don't want to take that girl off her work. Pity there are no children of her age around here."

May, when approached, readily agreed to take Ellen "out a race". And indeed it was like a race. Hand-in-hand, as soon as the washing-up was done, they raced away over the fields. May was a lively young country girl, only too happy to escape out of the gloomy old kitchen. She showed Ellen where to find birds' nests and where, if you stood very still, you could watch the rabbits nibbling along the edge of the barley field. One day she nearly caught a frog for her. "Pity," said May as the frog escaped, "you could've taken it back for your Auntie Jean," and they both fell about laughing. Ellen thought that May was the most wonderful person she had ever met in her whole life as, indeed, she probably was.

May slept in an attic room with a skylight, which you reached by a narrow stairway closed off from the landing by a door. It was always kept closed, and Ellen had been told not to go up there. She was curious about that door and a little anxious, thinking of Bluebeard. Then one day May, in her hurry to get ready, left the door open and Ellen followed her up.

"You can't see out," she said.

"You can, if you stand on the chair."

Ellen climbed up. "Oh, now I can see for miles and miles. I can see Scrabo. Wouldn't that be a lovely place to go?'

"Terrible long climb, but," said May.

From her vantage point Ellen turned round and surveyed May's room.

"Why do you have that picture there?" she asked.

"That one? That's the sacred heart of Jesus, child."

"I think it's horrible, all torn up like that."

"Child dear, you mustn't say things like that."

Ellen felt she had offended May. "But I like the one over your bed."

"It's not for you to be saying what you like or you don't like." May still sounded put out, and Ellen bit her lip. Then, in a softer voice, May said, "That's the Blessed Virgin that my Mammy gave me when I left home. She said if I said a prayer to her every night, she'd watch over me."

"And do you?"

"Every night before I go to sleep."

Ellen considered this. "Sometimes I feel awfully frightened in the dark. Do you think if I said a prayer to her she'd watch over me too?"

"Just you stick to the prayers your Mammy taught you."

"But would she?"

"Here, come you down off there. It's time we were away." And they scampered down the narrow stairs and out of the house. They raced away up the hill at the back and into the wood where primroses grew. They picked bunches and bunches.

As they came out on to the road Ellen said, "Oh, look, someone's dropped a primrose and it's been trodden on. The poor little thing."

At the top of the hill they stopped to look at the view. "Scrabo looks awfully near," said Ellen. "Couldn't we go sometime?"

"Listen, I'll tell you what we'll do. If the mistress allows it, I'll take you on my bike on my next day off, if it's fine that is."

"Oh, May, would you?"

Ellen, primroses in hand, dashed into her mother's room.

"Oh Mummy, May says she'll take me to Scrabo if you'll allow it. Do say 'yes', please."

Auntie Jean was not there that day. "I don't see why not. It's very good of May to offer."

"Oh goody, goody!" and she was off towards the kitchen. In the hall her father had just come back from business. "Mummy says we can go," she said as she sped past him.

"Where to?" he asked.

"Scrabo," and the kitchen door slammed behind her.

"What on earth's come over Ellen?" he said as he entered his wife's room, "She used to be such a quiet little mouse."

His wife smiled. "She's happy," she said and leant contentedly back on her pillows.

He went over to the window, thoughtfully stroking his nose, a habit he had when trying to put some difficult matter into words.

"You don't think," he said, "that we're letting her be too much with May?"

"What makes you say that?"

"Reverend Anderson stopped me today. Said he'd seen her several times hanging round the chapel."

"Probably waiting for May to come out."

"You know what they say – 'give us a child until he is seven'."

"But you don't believe that rubbish."

Her husband said nothing but remained at the window, thoughtfully stroking his nose.

That night when Ellen was in bed, her father came up to her room. He sat on the bed and asked her about her day. It seemed as if he meant to say something to her, but didn't get round to it. He stood up when she said her prayers, he stood with his hands in his pockets and she could hear him clinking his coins and his keys. He seemed to be thinking of something else. Then he kissed her goodnight and turned off the light. The landing light threw his enormous shadow on the ceiling, but this time she did not feel frightened. Putting her hands together, she addressed herself to the Lady in Blue in May's room and then, dreaming of the coming trip to Scrabo, she fell contentedly asleep.

The following Thursday, May's afternoon off, was one of those breathlessly still days in late spring when shafts of sunlight moved like spotlights over the little rounded hills and fields of County Down, here and there lighting up a brilliant patch of colour which would fade again as the shadow of the big, slow-moving clouds advanced. Ellen, perched on the pillion, hugged May's waist as they sped along the road. When they reached the base of Scrabo she eagerly helped push the bike up the rough road. They had to stop several times for a rest, and each time the view became more and more splendid. At last they reached the top. Her mother had given them money for tea, and this they ordered before beginning the climb to the top of the tower. Ellen thought the top would never come. Round and round and round. But at last they stepped out into the chill air on the parapet and looked about them. There stood the Mournes, looking very blue and majestic, and between lay the chequered field of County Down; below Newtownards was laid out like a map with Strangford Lough gleaming still and silver, and beyond the Isle of Man and Scotland, and round on the other side Divis and the Cavehill above the murky haze that was Belfast.

And then they came down, round and round, until Ellen's legs ached. They almost fell into the room at the bottom where the little range gave out a welcoming heat, and they ate homemade scones and apple cake and drank their tea. Then they whizzed down the hill, May gripping the handlebars and Ellen gripping May for dear life.

"Oh Mummy, we've been on top of the world," said Ellen as she burst into her mother's room, her face radiant.

"I'll be off now, ma'am," said May, "I've left everything ready for Miss Jean just to put in the oven."

"Thank you, May. And thank you for taking Ellen." Auntie Jean inclined her head. "She's not a peaky little thing now," said her mother, "quite a bit of colour in her cheeks." Auntie Jean said nothing.

All through their evening meal Ellen wanted to chatter on about the events of the day.

Auntie Jean and her father said, "Yes, that was nice," or "Really?" They did not seem interested. Instead Auntie Jean kept going on about something somebody had said in that boring old Council, and how her father should not let them get away with it. "If you give way once, they'll only ask for more. You mark my words." Funny how she was always asking people to mark her words. And also she was always giving this one or that one "a piece of my mind". Ellen wondered how she would look without it. Would there be a hollow or maybe a hole? Then she saw Auntie Jean looking at her and she whipped the smile off her face. Ellen was quite glad when it was time for her bed.

"Funny little thing, that daughter of yours," said Auntie Jean, after Ellen had gone. "Sometimes you see her smiling to herself, and you wonder what is going on inside that little head."

Auntie Jean stood over her as she had tucked her in. "And you're not to be silly and pretend you're frightened of the dark tonight," she said.

"Oh no, I'm not frightened any more. Every night I say a prayer to the Blessed Lady and she watches over me."

"You do WHAT?"

Ellen was surprised how Auntie Jean's eyes seemed to pierce right into her. "May has a picture of a lady in a blue veil," she began to explain.

"I see," snapped Auntie Jean. She turned quickly without kissing her goodnight and, switching off the light, went brusquely into her mother's room.

"She doesn't understand about us," Ellen confided to the

Lady. And then she told her about the idea of putting a frog in her lap, and her small body squirmed with delight at the thought. Soon she was happily asleep.

"That girl's got to go," announced Auntie Jean.

"For dear sakes, why?"

"I'll tell you why," and she did, at length. "I warned you how it would be when you engaged that girl."

"Ellen will be terribly upset," said her mother.

"It won't be easy to find a replacement," said her father.

"Well, if that's all that matters to you . . . " said Auntie Jean. "I can't think, if this got out," she rounded on her brother, "it would enhance your position in the Lodge."

So it was that about two weeks later Ellen was sent to spend the day with Auntie Jean, something she found very boring. As soon as she got back she raced round the house and in by the kitchen door. The kitchen was empty.

"Where's May?" she asked as she entered her mother's room.

"She's gone," said her father shortly.

"Where to?"

"She's gone away," said her mother, "we thought we'd like to have a different maid," her eyes imploring the child's forgiveness.

Ellen looked at them both, then turned her back and silently left the room. Very quietly she crept up the narrow stairs into May's room. The skylight was open and a chill draught filled the room. The mattress had been turned back and fresh sheets lay folded on the chair. But everything belonging to May had gone, the Lady in Blue, everything. Then she crept down the stairs and into the silent kitchen. The back door, which she had not bothered to close, was swinging in the wind, and the whole place felt cold and empty. She sat down on the step and buried her face in May's scratchy old apron.

THE MINSTREL BOY

As the rector solemnly read the names from the War Memorial plaque in the porch, Mrs Plunkett-Keane looked round at the congregation and wondered how many, if any, could remember the men to whom the names belonged. The congregation was not large, mostly elderly women like herself, demurely devout on this sad day, occupying pews formerly filled by so many of Mrs Plunkett-Keane's friends and acquaintances. Today she saw no one she knew.

During the rector's sermon she allowed her mind to slip away into wishful daydreaming: the fun it had all been, the tennis parties, the dances, the amateur dramatics, but as she left the church, she shook the rector's hand and thanked him for his sermon of which she had heard not a word.

Rather than go directly home to her lonely lunch, she thought she would walk along by the river and enjoy the fine autumn sunshine.

A small boy on a bench was idly kicking stones into the water.

She paused at a spot, where as children she and her brothers used to net "sprickly-backs", when a small stone hit her leg.

"I'm sorry, ma'am. I didn't mean to hit you."

"You'll destroy your boots if you kick stones like that," said Mrs Plunkett-Keane, never slow to admonish correction.

The child said nothing, but savagely kicked another stone.

"Is something wrong?" said Mrs Plunkett-Keane.

The child sniffed and shook his head, but Mrs Plunkett-Keane had seen the tears. She was a kindly woman.

"I think there is. Maybe if you told me, I could help."

He again shook his head, then straightening up, blurted out "It's me birthday."

"Well, this seems a funny way to celebrate a birthday."

"It's them Rogans," he said, "she never liked me, nor any of the rest of them, but Mr Rogan was always very decent. Ye see, him and me Da were in the war together and after me Da was killed, he used to give me half-a-crown regular every Christmas and asked me out here on my birthday. But the last year he died," he paused and sniffed. "I saved up and sent them a lovely card, but nothing ever came back . . . and to-day when I went, they'd gone and never left a note nor anything, just gone."

"So you have had no dinner?"

He shook his head.

"Any money?"

"Me fare back, but if I blow that I'd have to walk home."

"And where are you from?"

"St Brendan's on the North side."

"Long walk." She thought for a moment. Even if she gave him the money, there was nowhere round here which could give the child a decent square meal. He would only stuff himself with chips and Coke. "Look," she said, "if you came home with me, I think we could find you some dinner."

He raised his head and for the first time looked at her, half-doubting that she was serious about the invitation. She thought he was going to refuse. Then suddenly he smiled and nodded.

Mrs Plunkett-Keane lived in one of those Victorian terraces where the houses appear to be fairly low two-storey buildings, but actually have three storeys, the bottom one being sunk in a semi-basement. They are well set back from the road with sizable gardens and a flight of twelve or more steps leading up to an imposing front door.

The door with its glittering brass was opened by Kitty and an ecstatic little dog.

"This young fellow has missed his dinner – he can tell you his sorry tale himself – but I think if you take him down to the kitchen we'll be able to find something to keep hunger at bay. Mind he washes his hands before he sits down," she called after them and turned into her empty sitting room with the welcoming dog.

It was a room which had changed little since Mrs Plunkett-Keane had first entered it as an infant in her Nanny's arms. It had seen her and her brothers grow up, go out into the world, return with their spouses and offspring. She could remember when they'd had to put a leaf in the dining-room table, but now she never used that room. It seemed silly to sit alone at that big table, and she preferred Kitty to bring her a tray at the fireside. However, hearing the subterranean rumblings of the hoist, she rose and slipped through the sliding doors without waiting for Kitty to announce, as if it were a banquet, "Luncheon is served, ma'am."

She carved three generous portions and one lesser one for herself. She really wondered why she bothered with a joint on Sundays, but it would never have seemed like Sunday without one. She added roast potatoes in a similar ratio and a dollop of cauliflower. Then, as the joint under its vast dish-cover trundled down to the nether regions again, she preceded Kitty with the tray to the fireside.

"When that young fellow has finished his dinner, you can send him up," she said.

"Well, did you enjoy your dinner?" she said when he appeared.

"I did indeed, ma'am. The ladies below were very kind. Give me second helps of everything." Mrs Plunkett-Keane smiled to herself at how generous your servants could be with what was not really theirs to give. He sat gingerly on the edge of his chair and looked round him.

"Is them holy pictures?" he asked, gazing at some rather dim Victorian lithographs.

"No, that's the old Irish Parliament before the Union and we started to send MPs to Westminster. They are not very colourful, I'm afraid. One of my forefathers was a member, that's why I keep them there."

"A member of the Dail?"

"It wasn't called that then." He looked at her and considered she must really be very old indeed.

Kitty came up with the coffee and he watched fascinated as Mrs Plunkett-Keane nipped a sugar lump with the tongs and put it in her cup.

"Isn't that the cutest wee article! Just what you'd put coal on the fire with, only it's so tiny."

She nipped another lump. "Like one?" and dropped it into his hand. "Bad for your teeth, you know," but he only grinned as he crunched. He felt he was getting on quite well with this old bird.

"That's Mrs Wishart on the phone for you. ma'am," said Kitty and then as her mistress left the room, she stayed behind. As she explained later, "Just to keep an eye on that young lad. He was over here fiddling with the sugar tongs and then the things on your desk. 'Who's that guy?' says he. That guy! Did you ever hear the like? Says I, 'That is madam's husband and you don't call him that guy.' – 'He has a queer wheen of medals on him. Was he a general or something?' 'He was a *Major-General*', says I." Mrs Plunkett-Keane smiled at Kitty's triumphant tone, obviously thinking a Major-General topped all.

Alone again with Mrs Plunkett-Keane he said, "The other lady said he was your husband."

"That's right."

"He fought for the British, didn't he? And you think he done right?"

"Of course."

"You see, there's some blokes in the Home who take it out on me. They think my father was all wrong to have fought for the British, that you're not Irish if you do a thing like that."

"But he wasn't fighting for the British; he was fighting against Hitler. And you can tell your pals things might have been very different for us here, if people like him and others like him hadn't stood up to Hitler."

"They think anybody who helped the Brits is just plain daft."

"That's rubbish," snapped Mrs Plunkett-Keane almost crossly.

"You have to mind what you say in front of them. They heard me asking how you got to Islandbridge, and they were down on me at once."

"Did you want to go there?"

"I thought the Rogans might have been going. They have a truck."

"I have a car," she thought for a moment, "but I have never been to the place. I heard it was shockingly neglected and vandalised.

"They say it's been cleaned up."

"Let's go," she said. He was surprised at the almost girlish enthusiasm of the old girl.

"Well, I never did," said Kitty as she and Mary watched the pair of them with the dog at their heels going down the garden path towards the garage.

"I'm telling you," said Mary, "We have a stray cat, a dog from the shelter and now a waif in off the streets. Next it will be one of them black babies."

"Dear help her," said Kitty. "I'm sure she's lonely sitting up there, her lone the livelong day."

When they reached Islandbridge, Mrs Plunkett-Keane was pleased to see quite a number of people were laying poppies. She bought four little crosses from a man at the gate, one for her husband and one each for her brothers, and handed the fourth to the boy, who seemed to be searching for something inside his shirt.

"Couldn't let them see I had one of them on me," he grinned as he produced a rather tattered poppy and planted it with his cross. Then to her surprise he stood up straight and saluted, with the tail of his shirt, which had been pulled out with the poppy, fluttering in the wind.

* * *

Mrs Plunkett-Keane returned to her lonely life. She went to tea with some of her old friends, but as they had given up their cars, they never came to tea with her. When spring came, she offered to take them out for a drive, but some preferred to wait for the warmer weather, as they said. "The trouble with my friends," she said to Kitty, "is they're all so old." Kitty smiled to herself, knowing they were the same age as her mistress.

And if truth were told, some were a little anxious of being driven by Mrs Plunkett-Keane. Sometimes she missed the turning and had to reverse which led to embarrassing scenes with angry motorists hooting their horns.

Gradually she did not go to church so regularly, but she never failed on Remembrance Sunday, and each year she would walk back along the river. She often thought about the boy, and hoped that he still had the courage to honour his father's memory.

Then one day Kitty announced, "There's a young person wants to see you, ma'am." Kitty was deadly accurate in her definition of a young person or a young gentleman.

"What's he want?" said Mrs Plunkett-Keane. "Is he selling something?"

"He wants to speak to you, ma'am," smiled Kitty.

"You'll maybe not remember me," grinned a pleasant young man.

It was the grin she remembered. "My goodness, how you have grown. You're almost as tall as Kitty," and she held out her hand.

Kitty smiled as she left the room, bent on bringing the news to Mary.

"You've obviously left the Home, so what are you doing with yourself?"

"Oh, I left that place over a year ago. They got me a job in a draper's, but I don't think I'll be there much longer. It's desperate dull. No, I've ganged up with some others in a pop group. We call ourselves The Minstrels, and I'm the lead singer. All last winter we were performing at discos all round Dublin. Last month we were in Cork and next month we're going up north."

"Is that wise? They seem to do such dreadful things up there."

"It'll be all right. You see, one of the brothers used to talk a lot about how if only young people from both sides of the border could get to know each other, there wouldn't be all this hatred. And he has a friend up north who thinks the same, and he has booked us into two discos and we're to stay the night in a Catholic school. It'll be all right. I just thought I'd let you know, next Thursday at 11 p.m. we will be on RTE."

"That's awfully late."

"They don't give you peak time, not until you're a really big noise."

"Well, I hope you'll soon be a big noise, for 11 p.m. is long past my bedtime. Meantime my congratulations and best wishes."

She peeped through the window and watched as he walked away, a slim young figure almost military in his bearing, his head held high and his step assured and purposeful, full of confidence as he moved towards the new life which was opening before him.

"The minstrel boy to the wars has gone," she murmured and then suddenly felt sad.

* * *

On next Thursday at precisely 10.55 p.m., Mrs Plunkett-Keane in her dressing-gown returned to her sitting room and, huddling over the dying embers of the fire, turned on her wireless. And below in the kitchen Kitty and Mary, also in their night attire and overcoats sat close up to the still warm range and turned on theirs, too.

What they heard, none of them liked.

At breakfast next morning Kitty said, "Well, it wasn't really our sort of music, ma'am."

"Nor mine either," said Mrs Plunkett-Keane. "Far too loud and that drum just thumping away."

"But some of his songs were nice. I liked the one about the wee lad on his birthday who'd gone to visit his friends who had gone away and forgotten about him."

"Yes," said Mrs Plunkett-Keane, "but some of the others were such awful sentimental whinges about somebody, their girlfriend or somebody who'd let them down. Nothing but a bleat about poor me."

* * *

Some weeks later Kitty, looking very distressed, entered the drawing room without even knocking, the evening paper in her hand. "Were you listening to the news, ma'am?"

"No," snapped Mrs Plunkett-Keane, distinctly annoyed at being disturbed.

"Flanagan's boy come with the potatoes and he had the paper with him and he says, isn't that desperate?

She placed the paper on Mrs Plunkett-Keane's lap, who began to read it slowly without seeming to understand what she read. It said: "A pop group from Dublin who had just fulfilled two engagements in Lurgan and Craigavon was heading down the dual carriageway in their van towards Newry, when it was overtaken by another fast-moving vehicle. Shots were fired into the van and it is thought the driver was hit. The van then crashed and overturned. The occupants were all rushed to hospital, but were found to be dead on arrival."

Mrs Plunkett-Keane sat as if stunned.

"That nice young fellow," sobbed Kitty, "why did this have to happen? What harm has he ever done?"

"It's hard to know why these things happen," said Mrs Plunkett-Keane. "What good does it do anyone, shooting innocent young people?" Then she lent back in her chair and made as if to say something further, but her mouth only twitched.

"I think we'd better get the doctor," Kitty said to Mary, and when the doctor came, he pronounced that Mrs Plunkett-Keane had had a severe stroke and must go into hospital. Next morning his secretary phoned to say she regretted to tell them that Mrs Plunkett-Keane had passed away peacefully during the night.

"God rest her soul," said Kitty. And to Mary she said, "Och, God help her, she had no one left to live for."

THE WIND IS RISING

Normally this was the time of day I liked best, the evening light draining the colour from the garden, the trees and the fields beyond. Far away the mountains always seemed to look bluer before they faded from sight. It was all so peaceful, the silence only broken by a few laggard rooks returning to their rookery.

The soft night wind stirred the curtain, and I shivered.

"Shall I shut the window?"

"Yes, thank you," said my aunt.

The clock in the hall chimed the hour.

In the quiet of the house it seemed that the clock was ticking inside my brain. Yet, as I listened I scarcely heard it, for my ears strained out like feelers through the sound of the clock, the creaks of the old house, the hissing trees outside in the darkness, right down in imagination to the turn of the road at the bridge. But nowhere could they hear the sound of a car.

"Your uncle's late tonight," remarked my aunt, smoothing her needlework.

"Yes," I said, "they're trying those IRA men."

We both knew that perfectly well, yet my aunt showed no anxiety. With unhurried precision she selected a new shade, threaded her needle and began again. Perhaps to her this was just a common murder trial. But this was absurd. She had lived here with my uncle all through "the Troubles", and she probably knew more about the IRA than I did. Then how could she sit there complacently sewing...? Of course, she did not know of that letter. It had looked just like a dirty scrap of paper lying in the hall until I picked it up and read its sinister scrawlings. Perhaps she did know; if my uncle really got letters like that as often as he said he did, she must know. Perhaps she too would laugh it to scorn. Then why did he say not to tell her?

With hypnotic fascination I watched her needle darting deftly in and out of a rosebud. I did not wish to alarm the old lady unnecessarily, but I must tell someone soon. Childish threats may look ridiculous enough in the morning sunlight, but now it was different. The house seemed isolated, somehow, by the darkness and the quiet hissing of the trees.

"It's coming on nicely, isn't it?" asked my aunt, conscious of my stare.

"Yes," I said. "Aunt Ellen, Uncle Mark's never as late as this usually?"

"No, dear, not usually. But, you know, your uncle's a terrible gossip."

"But he'd never stay gossiping all this time, Aunt Ellen," I said again, "don't you think we should ring up?"

"If you like, dear. The phone's behind you."

I turned round and grasped the receiver. It was a relief to do anything, however futile. I waited for the operator to answer.

"They're always half-asleep," I grumbled, tapping the receiver rest. "Hello ... hello ... waken up there please... hello, I say..." Then a horrible realization began to creep up my spine: the line was quite, quite dead. I must try quickly to bluff the old lady.

"The line is dead, is it?" she asked quickly.

"Yes," I stammered.

"Then it's probably been cut," she said, rising. "Come, my dear, we may not have much time, and there are some things I shouldn't like them to get."

I rose numbly.

"We'll take the Gainsborough first." she went on, "and put it in the cellar. And then you go to the library and fetch your uncle's first editions – he is so fond of them – and when you have done that, dear, come upstairs, I shall have more for you to carry."

I listened and marvelled. My own brain seemed petrified, but I was glad to be active at last and thankful that the age-long spell of waiting and listening was broken.

As I carried down my aunt's neatly packed personal treasures, I realized that she could not possibly have packed them in the time and that she must have had them ready for years past.

"Aunt Ellen," I said, "did you know Uncle Mark got a threatening letter this morning?"

"Well, dear, I always suspect if he kissed me goodbye several times over, he's had something of the sort. I'm glad James took today instead of his usual Thursday," she went on when I returned for another load, "it doesn't do to show them what you anticipate."

"Them?" James Kernoghan one of "them"? I glanced at her, but she showed no trace of bitter suspicion. It was absurd of me to doubt old James. Yet it was strange that for no apparent reason he should change his day out; it was also strange how that letter "blew" into the hall.

"And this shawl of your Great-aunt Eleanor's," said my aunt, "I know these things aren't of much actual value, still, to me they're irreplaceable."

I should like to have entered James's room to see if he had packed his bags and abandoned us. Such things had happened before in Ireland. When I thought of James's devotion to us, I was instantly ashamed of myself.

Feverishly I worked, collecting, carrying and stowing away in the cellar, It was an odd-looking little jumble, squatting amongst the bottles and the mildewed croquet set, a pathetic anthology of human joys. My great-grandmother's fragile tea set; several pictures, leaning drunkenly; a jewel box; some bundles of old silver; piles of fusty hide-bound books; an indistinct photo with some war medals in a frame; a delicate fan and a silver-mounted horse's hoof.

"Well, that's all we can do," said my aunt, "we don't want to arouse their suspicion by leaving the place too empty. They'll be quite safe here. Even if the house is burned down, we can always burrow in through that grating."

"You think they'll burn it?"

"My dear, I'm taking no chances. Remember they only gave poor Major Repton five minutes to get out, and he lost everything, his priceless manuscripts and all. . . . Well now, we mustn't let them catch us down here."

"Shall I draw the curtains?" I asked, as we entered the drawing room again.

"No thank you, dear, we'll try to behave as we do every night."

We sat down and my aunt resumed her work. As I sat waiting and listening once more, my back to the windows, I was conscious of the blackness of the night outside, It seemed that the shadowy trees had crept nearer the house as if to smother it, and out of the tail of my eye I could see the yellow orb of the lamp reflected in the windows. It was reflected in varying shapes in each of the square panes, and each reflection was a lemon-like evil eye watching us.

"I'm fond of that spinet, too," said my aunt, "but I'm afraid there's no room for it in the cellar."

I looked round the room at all the familiar objects, and as I looked I felt I must have gone mad. It was incomprehensible that men should burst into this room in a short while and destroy everything, all those things which meant so much to us and nothing to them. And we sat waiting for them to come.

"The wind is rising," said my aunt.

My mind wandered back to the turn of the road. It was always a bad corner, and all cars slowed down to take it. I could see the thick hedge on the left-hand side looking dark and menacing, the splitting flash and stab of a bullet... I wondered what they would do afterwards. The river was very convenient, but then the car might be useful to them. Perhaps they would use it to come up here.

Then all my nerves stiffened. A car was coming up the drive. I glimpsed its lights as it turned in at the gate. Then it swept on into the yard. I had not expected them to attack from the rear. I had pictured a dramatic encounter on the front door steps.

Then there followed a period of complete silence. I wondered if they were surrounding the house. Perhaps the house was already surrounded, and these were the chiefs. I wondered if I ought to stand up. It seemed rather ignominious to be shot sitting down, and besides I had always thought the cretonnes pretty. But if they were going to burn the whole place anyway, I supposed the cretonnes no longer mattered.

Then the back door slammed and deliberate steps echoed up the passage. I rose to my feet. "Just remain seated, dear," said my aunt, "remember who you are."

My heart was thumping hotly in my ears and somewhere down behind my knees. Then a sudden, nerve-shattering sound split my head. It was so close, it seemed inside my ears.

"Answer it, dear," said my aunt.

"Hello, can you hear me?" said a voice, "We're just testing the line. Sorry you've had such a bad breakdown."

"Not a word to your uncle, dear," said my aunt, "he hates to think I've been fussy."

"Sorry I'm late," said my uncle, "got talking to old Renshaw. Haven't seen him for years."

"We've left you a bit of cold chicken on the sideboard," said my aunt.

"No thanks, I've eaten."

"I'll put it back in the fridge," I said and hurried from the room. I did not want them to see I was in tears.

THE DIRECTOR-GENERAL'S WIFE

This story dates from the time when Robinson & Cleaver's shop occupied the corner block opposite the City Hall in Belfast. It had a magnificent marble staircase, and customers descending from the first floor could overlook the whole of the ground floor and feel that they really were the monarchs of all they surveyed.

Mrs Ferguson's face lit up as she entered the dining room on this pleasant sunlit afternoon. As well it might, for it was a pleasant room looking out across Belfast Lough from its position high up above Craigavad. A quick glance reassured her that Marleen had laid the table correctly, everything was in its place, but with a faint sigh once again she regretted that she did not possess a silver candelabra instead of those glass things. Still, if all went well tonight, and she hoped it would, maybe Charles could be persuaded.

She considered the placing of her guests, three women and five men, which was awkward. Mr John Martin, the Director-General, the D-G as she called him, was unmarried. Charles, of course, would be at the head of the table, and between him and the D-G she would place Mrs Belinda Wilson Foster, whom she considered to be a real acquisition for her party. She was so lively, so charming, knew everyone in Craigavad and possessed really beautiful diamonds which she did not hide under the table. Her husband, Major Wilson

Foster, was a bit of a bore, some people thought, but still, a military title would show the D-G that they were not all plumber's mates. He need never know that Wilson was the Major's Christian name and not a double-barrel. And then there were Mr McDade and Mr and Mrs McKinstry. She had asked Charles "Must we have them?" and he had said yes. They were the last surviving partners of a small concern supplying plumbers' materials, which through its lack of enterprise had somehow missed the post-war boom in central heating and was in decline when Charles had joined it as a young man. Then a takeover bid had come from England and Charles had been made managing director. An upstairs storeroom had been converted into a brilliant showroom displaying a glittering array of bathroom furnishings, and business had revived.

She would put Mrs McKinstry on Charles's other side and old Mr McDade beside her. Mrs McKinstry had three topics of conversation, the weather, the price of everything and the "carry-on" of young people nowadays. After that she would lapse into a disapproving silence. But that would not matter much, for Mr McDade was slightly deaf and would probably find it a relief. She herself would be at the bottom of the table with Mr McKinstry and the Major on either hand.

She gave a last approving glance over her table. She hoped someone would notice how exactly the white shading to pink of the candles matched the white shading to pink of the roses. "That's Ophelia," she heard herself saying, "a lovely old-fashioned rose with a heavenly scent. I brought it with me from my old home." Mr Martin did not know where her old home was, but it suggested a lovely old house in the country, surrounded by Ophelias and Gloire de Dijon, the flower beds edged with little tufts of mignonettes and forget-me-nots. Which was not the case.

Crossing the hall, she caught sight of herself in the mirror.

Yes, that little woman in Holywood had done her hair very well. She felt well pleased with life.

The phone rang. "This is the hospital. Mrs Foster is sorry she won't be able to be with you to-night." "Oh, my God," she gasped. "No, it's not that serious. She fell over the step and has sprained her ankle badly, but we want to take an X-ray and we'll keep her in overnight." Only after she put the receiver down did she realize that she had never sent any messages of regret or sympathy. Perhaps she should ring back. She was so upset, she was near to tears. No, she would enquire in the morning. Instead she rang Charles and exploded her troubles all over him.

"Never mind, dear, it isn't the end of the world."

"But I so wanted this evening to be a success."

"I know you did, dear. And maybe it will be."

"What, with those two old duffers – three if you count the Major."

"Old McDade is a nice old pet."

"Thank heavens, he's a widower. Two Mrs McKinstrys in one evening would be the end."

"Don't take it so much to heart. I'll be home as soon as I can."

"And don't forget, you have to call for my necklace at Robinson & Cleaver's. They're fixing the catch. I want to wear it to-night with my new dress."

* * *

As he waited at the counter for the girl to bring him the necklace, he thought a child's ball had touched his foot, but picking it up, he found it was an orange. And looking round there were many more oranges coming hoppity-hop down the beautiful staircase. All around people were diving under chairs and behind counters retrieving oranges, whilst a voice he recognized from his childhood was saying,

"Oh thank you, thank you so much, so kind, thank you all."

"May I?" he asked, offering his orange.

"Oh Charlie, bless you."

"Thank you, thank you so much," she continued to her helpers. Then under her breath, "Dear Heaven, I wish the ground would open and swallow me. Oh dear!" as a couple of oranges hopped out of her arms.

"Here," he said severely, "put the rest into my briefcase, before you start the whole thing all over again. People will think you're advertising the oranges." He laughed.

"It's not funny."

"May I give you a lift home?"

"Now that's different. That would be really kind instead of standing there laughing your head off."

He tried to look serious as they hurried away, but as the swing doors closed behind them, they both burst into uncontrollable laughter.

They were old friends. They had grown up together in one of the quieter, respectable, but not particularly affluent areas of Knock in East Belfast, but since his marriage they had not seen much of each other. Mrs Charles Ferguson did not consider Molly McKibbin a desirable social asset. She had no car, and if you invited her, there was always so much fuss about getting someone to bring her and return her.

"You're looking well, Charlie," said Molly. "Married life seems to agree with you." He smiled, but said nothing. "And how is your good lady?" she continued. She always addressed Edna like that.

"Bit of a tizzy at the moment. The boss is over from England about the possible expansion of the business, and Edna thought she would have a nice little dinner party for him. She managed to capture one of the local socialites for his entertainment and now the woman has broken her ankle, and we're left with her bore of a husband and the two old directors with one fuddy-duddy wife that I insisted be asked. We were one woman short before, the boss has no wife, but now we are two short – I say, are you doing anything to-night? Oh, I know it's a very backhanded invitation, asking you to fill in at the last moment but honestly, it would save the day for me."

"But not for your good lady. If she wants a replacement for a social lioness, I'd be no help to her."

"Rubbish. You're always so good at talking to all sorts of people. Do come. Otherwise it's going to be the most ghastly evening."

Molly thought for a moment, and then with a little smile said, "On the contrary. I think it might be rather amusing."

* * *

"Is that you, Charles?" Edna called from the sitting room. "Have you got my necklace?" The phone began to ring. "It's in my briefcase," he said, dumping the case in the sitting room and going to the phone.

"What on earth are all those oranges doing in your case?" Edna asked when he returned.

"Good heavens, she's left them behind. Never mind, she can get them tonight."

"Who's left them behind?"

"Molly McKibbin, you remember? She lived next door in Knock. I ran into her in Robinson & Cleaver's," and he related the incident. Edna said, "Which I suppose you both thought was awfully funny."

"It was, really."

"And what do you mean that she can collect them to-night?"

"Molly Mckibbin is just about the one and only person we could ask at such short notice. I knew how stuck you were for another female, so I asked her."

"That just about makes my day. Charles, how could you? Here am I trying to do my best to further your career, trying to impress the D-G and you go and invite that nonentity."

"She's not a nonentity," he said quite sharply. "She may not be a social asset, but she's not a nobody."

"You'll never understand, Charles."

"Probably not," he snapped. "It's not dinner jackets, is it?"

"I didn't think the other Directors would have any."

"Thank heavens for that. All the same – think I'd better have a wash and brush-up. That was Molly on the phone. She'd got herself a lift to Holywood, and I said I would pick her up at the Maypole at a quarter to."

* * *

The McKinstrys with old McDade arrived first.

"Very kind of you to invite us to meet the Director," smiled Mrs McKinstry. She attempted to sit upright in one of the deep armchairs but, finding it difficult, remained perched unsteadily on the edge.

Edna hastened to explain that Charles had gone to fetch a guest who had no car, but hoped he would be back at any minute. They exchanged views about the weather and then, to Edna's relief, she heard the doorbell. This time it was the Major. He threw a quick glance over the others to see if they were people he knew, should know or would like to know. Dismissing them on all three counts, and barely listening to their names as they were introduced, he allowed himself to be smothered in Edna's effusions about his wife's mishap.

And then there seemed to be a lot of confusion and laughter in the hall.

"No, no, I'm not Charlie's wife. I'm Molly McKibbin," and as she entered the room, she said, "I'm sorry, I'm the reason your host wasn't here to welcome you all. I have no car."

"And you are Mr Martin, our Director-General," said Edna to the man behind her and began making her introductions again.

"Pleased to meet you," beamed Mrs McKinstry, who in her effort to get out of her deep chair nearly fell at his feet.

"We're very pleased to have someone over from HQ looking us over," said her husband.

"And I am very impressed with what I've seen. Quite different from the first time I was here," said Mr Martin.

"Aye, and it's Charlie boy here that's made the difference," croaked old Mr McDade.

"Charles," said Edna with emphasis – she wished they would stop calling him Charlie – "Charles always likes to give of his best."

"That he does," nodded Mr McDade.

"And where is Charles now?" enquired Edna.

"Putting the car away."

So Edna began her introductions again. She felt furious that Charles had left her to do absolutely everything. And Molly just stood there relaxed and looking quite presentable for once in a plain black dress over which she had thrown a really lovely Indian shawl.

"Here are your oranges," said Edna curtly.

"Oh, good gracious! Did I leave them behind? The bag waited until I was just at the top of that staircase in Robinson & Cleaver's before it burst and all the oranges went down hoppity-hop."

"I thought it was some promotion stunt," said Charlie, coming in, "the return of Nell Gwynn."

"I just wanted to bolt out of the place."

"Very embarrassing, I'm sure," said Mrs McKinstry.

"But everybody was picking them up and handing them to me."

"And lucky you were, dear lady," said the Major. "Same thing happened to me in Cairo, but I didn't see any of my oranges again. Desperate thieves in the Middle East, and so quick. It's not that they don't know how to deal with them. If they catch a man stealing, they chop off his hand, chump like that," everyone gasped, "and if he does it again, they chop off his other hand, and that fixes him."

"I'm sure it would," said Charlie.

"Unless, of course, he used his feet," said Molly in such a gentle little voice, no one heard her – except the D-G, whose eye twinkled.

And so they all went in to dinner.

"That's a lovely rose," said the D-G.

"That's Ophelia, a lovely, old-fashioned rose that you can't get anymore. I brought it with me from my old home." She paused, hoping she had made the desired impression, but thought Molly was about to say something. Only Molly knew that the garden of her old home was a small rectangle fenced with iron railings in front of a terraced house in Ballyhackamore.

"I'm sure Ophelia appreciated the change," Molly smiled.

"Everything did," said Charlie. "I think it must be the air. It's very clear, bit breezy up here, but fresh."

Old Mr McDade, who so far had not spoken on anything, suddenly said, "My old mother always used to say, if you could smell the foreshore at Sydenham, the weather would be fine for three days," and now no one knew quite what to say to that.

Edna flustered, "But of course, up here we're far away from the foreshore."

"You must have a lovely view from here," said the D-G.

"Perfect," said Edna. She was tempted to say with a dramatic flash of her one ring "Divine', but feared that Molly might giggle.

"When the Tall Ships were here, it really was a tremendous sight," said Charlie. "Anything that could float swarmed out. You could almost think a floating carpet had been laid down round them."

"I saw some of these windsurfing fellows among them," growled the Major, "damned dangerous. Should never be allowed."

“I saw it all from the top of Knockagh,” said Molly, “it was wonderful. The tiny craft spread out from either shore like algae.”

“Like algae?” said Edna. “What a nasty idea!”

“I see what you mean,” said the D-G to Molly and smiled. He at least seemed to be enjoying the party. Edna was not.

“Our nephew who lives in Bangor on Princetown Road invited us for the day,” said Mrs McKinstry.

“I mind the time they ran a wee steamer from Queen’s Bridge ‘Bangor and Back for a Bob’ it was. Many’s the time we enjoyed that trip,” and Mr McDade withdrew again into his memories.

Again no one knew what to say next.

Edna was frightened they were going to start talking shop. “Are you over for long?” she asked the D-G.

“Only a few days. I felt like a break and there’s something I’ve wanted to do for years. As a child I liked the *Narnia* books – C.S. Lewis, you know – and this time I thought I’d hire a car and go round all the places he knew.”

“How nice of you,” said Molly, “our church worked out a nice little tour of the district to mark his centenary, but very few people came.”

“That was a shame.”

“Yes, I was quite looking forward to being a tour guide.”

“You wouldn’t care to guide me around?”

“With pleasure. It’s nice to meet anyone interested in C.S. Lewis. So many people seem to have forgotten him. He loved this part of the world. He and his brother did a lot of walking in the Holywood hills.”

“That’s just what I want to do.”

Edna wondered what on earth they were talking about. She felt she must introduce some more general topic. “Anything good in the pictures this week?”

“Damn all,” said the Major, “nothing but American trash.”

“*Swan Lake* is on at the Opera House,” offered Molly.

"Do you like ballet?" asked Mr Martin.

"Very much."

"And you?" he asked Edna with a peculiar smile.

"Oh yes, it's very nice, but really since we came to live up here, Belfast seems far away, and then it's always so difficult to park. Anyway, we've seen *Swan Lake*."

"But I always think, old as it is, it always bears seeing again."

"I wouldn't go to see one of them ballets, if you paid me," snapped Mrs McKinstry. "The idea of men pointing their toes! It's not right." When Mrs McKinstry snapped her mouth like that, it made her look as if she had forgotten to put in her teeth.

"They should follow some manly sport," growled the Major, "football or boxing, something like that, not skipping about to music."

There seemed to be nothing else to say and, as the guests eventually departed, Edna overheard Mr Martin offering to run Molly home. "Well, there's no accounting for taste," she said to herself.

* * *

Time passed and the plans for the new development progressed, but left Edna very much on her own. Mrs Wilson Foster never returned the invitation, her husband probably having given a horrendous account of the party she had missed. Thus, although Edna had spent much time and money on trying to learn to play bridge and golf, she sadly came to realize that these things were not for her.

And so, when premises were finally found in Ballymena, which was thought to be a good centre, and the suggestion that they should move nearer the business was made, she raised no objections. She was not really sorry to leave Craigavad and did not bother to dig up Ophelia.

When all was completed, it was decided to have a grand

formal opening and invite the Minister of Trade and Development. The Director-General was again coming over from England. This time he said he would be bringing his wife. Old Mr McDade had died and they had appointed two new directors in his place, Mrs McKinstry was having her hip replaced, so Edna felt she had no responsibilities for the social side of things. They could all have lunch together in a nearby hotel. She thought her costume, although not new, would do fine for the occasion.

"How nice to see you again," said Mr Martin. "I think you know my wife."

"Oh yes, indeed," said Molly, looking very smart, "it was in your house we met."

And after they had all gone away, Edna said. "Well, I never did."

DEATH ON DRUMNAHORK

"No, not this year," he said to his secretary as he prepared to leave, "I find those Mediterranean places a bit hot for me at my time of life. And the wife always loves Donegal, so this is her holiday this year." He did not add that there would be no more Mediterranean holidays for her after the disgraceful way she had behaved last time, fooling around with that young Italian gigolo chap. No, from this on it would be Donegal.

He hoped he would get some golf anyway. Some of his colleagues went there quite frequently and enjoyed the golf or the fishing, but on previous holidays Marjorie had always wanted him to climb some storm-blasted headland, bathe on some beach in tumultuous surf or creep into some smoky cottage to watch them practising some dying art, spinning by hand or weaving. She was ten years younger than he, and although she had unbounded energy, it was never directed towards any reasonable form of sport, she had so many other interests.

So they journeyed on in the car, rather silently, an ageing couple no longer interested in sex or maybe even in each other. The fault perhaps was his, but such a thought had never entered his head.

"Mmm," said Marjorie suddenly, "did you smell it? Peat. Always, when we came with Dad that was what told us the holidays had really begun. Even the dogs sat up and wanted to put a nose out of the window."

Her family always stayed in farmhouses, her father wanting to avoid the slot machines and candyfloss of other, more sophisticated seaside resorts. "All children need is a sandy beach, some rockpools to fish in and some other children," was what he said and what he gave them.

As they drew nearer their destination, Marjorie recounted events of her childhood, the hill where the brakes on John's bike had failed and he had gone over the hedge; the bay where Mary had been so painfully stung by a sea urchin. He listened, but without much interest, and heaved a sigh when at last they reached the little fishing hotel, where Marjorie had booked them in.

He got out stiffly and after a young man had relieved him of their suitcases, he turned aside into the bar, where some of the residents had already assembled, their catches displayed on the counter.

"Those yours?" one of them asked him, indicating two good trout on a plate.

"I don't fish," he said.

"Good God, what are you doing here?"

He felt disgruntled with the man. He took his whiskey and withdrew to the window seat. Marjorie joined him. "The Staffords are here," she said, "you remember them, don't you? We met them once at Mary's." Vaguely he thought he did. He collected fossils and she made pictures out of bits of Donegal tweed. Not much hope of golf there. "They say the boat is taking supplies out to the lighthouse tomorrow and that they are now allowed to take passengers if there's room. The Staffords are going, and I thought we might go too. I've always wanted to do that, but it was never possible before."

Well, he did not see much hope of golf, so he might as well. He only hoped it would not rain.

It did not rain the next day. The clouds and mists which had clung to the hills the previous evening gradually lifted, and then suddenly the sun burst through and Donegal was revealed in all its glory as dramatically as had a theatre curtain been drawn aside.

"Perfect," said Marjorie, taking a deep breath. The Staffords were equally enthusiastic, and they all moved off towards the harbour. It was not a large motor boat, but somehow everyone managed to squeeze on to a seat. Mr Stafford attempted to carry on a conversation with the boatman, but not much could be heard above the noise of the engine. The sea sparkled all around, the gulls screamed and swooped, and the little boat responded to the gentle swell. In less than an hour they were clambering out of the boat and up the steep stone steps of the lighthouse quay. An elderly keeper welcomed them and explained the functions of each department as they climbed the spiral staircase. Most of his visitors, finding the climbing strenuous, dropped off in the living quarters so that, when they reached the top storey, only Marjorie and the Staffords were with him. Here he explained there was always someone on look-out duty, and leaving them in the care of his colleague Michael Logue, he hurried down to his other guests. Marjorie thought Michael looked nice.

The Staffords were ecstatic about the view all around. How different it looked from the sea. And how far inland you could see. Michael opened the heavy door on to the surrounding platform, but although safely shielded by iron railings, they all shrank back. Seeing the ground so far below through the open slats of the floor made them dizzy.

"I'm sure you get some gales out here in the winter," said Mr Stafford.

"We do indeed, sir," said Michael, "there's times here when you can't see the mainland at all. Nothing but boiling seas and driving rain. There's a hole out there on the point, Sally-Anne's Hole they call it, and when she blows, she sends the spray hundreds of feet up as high as the lighthouse itself."

"You must lead a very lonely life out here," said Marjorie,

sidling closer to him. “No female companionship.” And she smiled.

“Aye, that’s true,” he said.

“You must miss that, surely.”

“I get home to the wife every three weeks.”

“You have a wife?”

“Aye, and two kids. I’ll be seeing them next Thursday in time for the fair. The kids can’t wait.”

Shouts came from below. It was time to go, and the Staffords made for the stairs.

“I’ll look out for you next Thursday,” murmured Marjorie quietly, as she squeezed past him.

For several minutes after they had gone he stared stupidly at the door. “I believe that woman was making a pass at me.” The thought amused him at first. No one had ever done that to him before. It gave him a kick. But then, a shy man, he felt embarrassed, ashamed of himself being involved in any such thing, and as the days went by and Thursday drew nearer, he became anxious and hoped that this peculiar woman was not going to spoil the day. He told himself that he had nothing to feel guilty about. Yet that was the feeling it left with him.

Marjorie meanwhile was enjoying her holiday, taking vigorous walks in all directions, revisiting the different bays and inlets of the rocky coast. The fairground was setting itself up with much shouting and commotion, and then suddenly the whole street was filled with booths selling everything imaginable. The steam organ made some alarming noises as it tuned itself in to burst forth with “Daisy, Daisy’. The fair was in full swing.

She bought a pair of handknitted socks for herself and a pair for Henry for his golf. To her relief, he had found someone he knew staying in the other pub and they proposed going over to Rosapenna on Thursday. “You won’t mind, if I leave you?” he had asked, “We’ll be away all day.” “I’ll be all right,” she said and smiled.

She paused beside all the little leprechauns with their shillelaghs and their shamrocks, and wondered who bought such hideosities; designed for the tourist, she supposed. She wandered on and hovered beside the religious objects, listening as the price of a rosary was haggled over. The price asked was 30p, the price offered 25p, and before it changed hands at 27p, a lot of ground had been covered, in the course of which the seller rounded on the buyer "And would ye sin yer soul for the sake of thruppence?"

Other boats were bringing people in from the islands and Michael mingled with them as they walked up from the harbour. He remembered the way she had said "I'll look out for you on Thursday", and the smiling way she had slithered round him in the doorway. He had taken the white top off his cap, and now he pulled the cap low over his nose. He hoped she would not be there, but dared not look up to see. He slipped round behind the houses and made off across the fields to his home. Molly flung her arms round him and he warmly returned the hug, kissing her again and again. "Get on with you," she laughed, "what are ye at in front of the children?" The boys wanted to sit on him, Rover jumped and barked, and the cat arched her back primly but remained on the windowsill. This was home. That woman was right when she said he must miss it.

"When can we go to the fair?" yammered the children.

"Whisht now and leave your Da in peace," said Molly. "He'll be wanting a bite of dinner in him, after the early start he's had."

And the moment the meal was over the yammering started again.

"You take them," he said.

"Me? What's the matter with you?"

"Och, I'd just be as happy here. All that noise and people pushing about."

"Ah go on, you're not that old. You've always enjoyed taking the boys before and it won't be the same for them if you're not there."

"Well, all right then," he said without much enthusiasm.

"You feeling all right?" she said, darting a quick look at him – she had never seen him like that before.

"I'm OK. Come on, boys," and they all set off.

"Why are we going this way?" asked Molly, as he led them along behind the houses.

"I thought we would do the amusements first."

"Oh goody, goody," chorused the children.

Usually he wore his uniform and Molly enjoyed parading down the street beside him. But today he had handed her his white top for washing, although as far as she could see it was spotless, and instead put on his old woolly cap and sweater, so that he was indistinguishable from all the other native seamen.

He indulged the kids with rides on the roundabout and the swings until Molly said, "Now that's enough or you'll have them seasick."

Reluctantly he turned towards the crowded street. "Can we have ice cream, Dad?"

"I don't know if there is any."

"I heard its wee tune. It must be there somewhere," said Molly. "Look, why don't you take the kids and I'll follow you. There's one or two things I want for the house." So they separated.

A cornet in each hand, he emerged from the throng around the ice-cream van. "So you did come." said a soft voice.

"Yes, I did," he almost snapped.

"You don't seem very happy this evening, do you?" And she sidled up to him, smiling.

"Can't you see, I've got my hands full? Here you are, boys."

"So bogged down with family duties. No time for anyone else. Too bad."

He saw Molly approaching, a milk jug in one hand and a large plate under her arm.

"This is my wife," he said desperately.

"Been doing some shopping," smiled Marjorie. "Well, I'll leave you to it," and she sidled away.

"Who on earth was that?" asked Molly.

"Some daft woman that came out to the lighthouse on a trip. I think she's looking for a man."

"Well, she's not having mine," and changing the milk jug to her other hand, she took his arm and squeezed it.

"I'm damn well sure she's not," he smiled down at her and, returning the squeeze, he kissed her.

"Shsh, people will be looking."

"Let them," he said and kissed her again.

They paused beside a stall selling footwear.

"Them's nice," said Molly, picking up a pair of sandals.

"Made in Taiwan," he said, "they'd probably fall to bits in the wet of this place."

"How much?" she asked.

"Do you really want them?"

"I like the cute wee square heel they have."

He made an offer, and after a little haggling he put the sandals in his pocket.

When they reached the "hotel' at the end of the street, Marjorie was standing in the doorway, a glass in her hand. "Time for a quick one?" she called.

"No thanks," he said.

"See you at the ceilidh to-night then."

He shook his head and they walked on.

"Pity. It could be fun." Her simpering tone suggested the sort of fun.

"Brazen hussy," he muttered.

"Indeed, I never seen the like," Molly said.

Once the fair had packed itself up and gone, the children were no longer interested in the village street. He had made them a kite and they spent their time running to and fro, trying to get it to fly, much to Rover's excitement. Michael was able to do some household jobs for Molly, and the few days of his leave passed all too quickly. Finally they all went together to the harbour to see him off. As he had been rather dreading, Marjorie was there too.

"Going so soon?" she said. "We've hardly seen anything of you since you came over. Never mind. We'll look out for you next year, and you can look out for us tomorrow. We're all going to climb the Boar's Snout, and I'll wave to you from there." She completely ignored Molly's blazing eyes.

From the boat he looked up once and waved to the children and then seemed engaged in talking to the boatman.

"Come, boys. I've work to do," said Molly and she hustled them away. That woman!

Every Friday she baked two wheaten farls, one for themselves and one for her old uncle Peter. He lived alone in the little cottage where he had reared his family, high up on the Boar's Snout, and despite all the advice and entreaties from his relatives, he refused to go into a welfare home. A few hens, a goat, a small patch of potatoes and a stack of peat supplied most of his needs, and Molly's weekly visit supplied the rest, which were not many. His daughters, one who was married in Derry, and the other in Enniskillen, sent him parcels occasionally, when they remembered, and the postman in his little van made the bumpy journey up the back of the Boar's Snout. Molly feared that some day someone would find the old man dead.

The village approved of Molly's attitude to her uncle: "If the old boy above there doesn't want to go into a home, his family has no right to make him," and frequently, as she set out, some little package would be dropped into her bicycle basket. "There's a few scones for your uncle's tea still warm off the griddle," or "There's a wee pot of my bramble jelly."

She usually left immediately after dinner, but today various things had kept her back and it was late in the afternoon when she finally got the boys cleaned up to be left at her mother's and she pushed her bike out only to find that its front tyre was flat. She never mended punctures, Michael always did that. If only she had looked at the bike before he had left yesterday. Woefully they went to Eamon in the garage. He was willing to do the job, but said it would not be fit to face such a bumpy road that evening. "Wait a minute," he said and popped next door, returning with a delivery boy's tricycle. "I thought they wouldn't be using it on a Saturday evening."

The boys delightedly hopped into the front basket and were delivered to their grandmother with hurried explanations. "You'll have to hurry back," she said, "if you're to get home before dark. That thing has no lights."

As she pedalled along the flat straight road towards the base of Drumnahork, she saw the sun sinking in a yellow watery sunset far out over the Atlantic, and when it finally sank into a large black cloud, an eerie sinister light was shed over the land. It was as if that great headland before her was just sitting there, brooding malignantly over the little village and its harbour.

Molly pedalled hard, but the tricycle had small wheels and she felt she was making poor progress, and when she came to the steep part, she had to get down and push. She heard a car approaching and almost thought of dumping the tricycle and hitching a lift, but as she half-turned, she caught a glimpse of the pale yellow anorak That Woman seemed to live in, and she turned no further. There were four of them in the car and she watched them park it where the road ended just below Uncle Peter's cottage, and start to climb the rough path that led round the head of Drumnahork and out on to what was commonly called the Boar's Snout.

Uncle Peter was standing at the open door.

"I thought you weren't coming," he said.

"Now, Uncle Peter, have I ever let you down?"

"No, child, that's true. You're the only one that bothers about your old uncle."

"Not the only one. There's a nice wee trout that Robert James left in for you last night. He said they were rising nicely up on Lough Beg."

"I'll wet the tea."

"I can't stay long."

"You can stay for a cup o'tea, before you go. The kettle's been singing this long time."

She smiled. Uncle Peter's kettle, as it hung above the open fire, was permanently singing. The tea was very welcome after her long push.

"Thanks a lot. But now I must be going."

Outside the darkness had increased, and from underneath the dark cloud which had spread out across the bay she could see the pale curtain of falling rain.

From the other side of the fuchsia hedge she heard voices, angry, exasperated voices.

"Sometimes she can be damned stubborn."

"But, really, I don't think we should have left her."

"Well, I did all I could. You heard me. Daft idea. Wanted to see the lighthouse beam sweep over the headland. Daft."

The voices continued until she heard the car doors slammed and they drove off.

So That Woman was still up there. Alone. Molly was curious to know what on earth she could be doing. There was a little path very much steeper than the one the others had followed, which led directly to the top, and, pushing the tricycle aside, she scrambled up. She reached the top just as the first beam swept round. And there a few feet below her at the very edge of the cliff was the yellow anorak, waving its arms and blowing kisses. Blowing kisses to my husband! A wild, uncontrollable rage consumed her as she rushed down.

* * *

Out on the lighthouse Michael had been doubtful about looking out for her, but as lighting-up time drew nearer, curiosity got the better of him and he climbed the stairs. His colleague was watching through the binoculars a small yacht trying to make the harbour.

"Holiday yachtsmen." he chuckled. "They never think of reefing until it's too late. They just don't seem to see the squalls coming until they are laid flat."

"Do we ring the lifeboat?"

"I think they will just make it now. The jib's drawing nicely, anyway."

Casually Michael watched as the beam passed over the familiar rocks and beaches, the harbour and the little white houses and then up over the higher cliffs to the Boar's Snout. There, he was not quite sure if he were glad or sorry, he saw the little yellow figure dancing up and down. He thought he saw another figure behind her, but the beam had passed on and when next it came round, there was no one there at all, only at the foot of the cliff some loose stones were splashing into the sea.

"Funny," he said to his colleague, "I thought I saw people on the Boar's Snout."

"Aye, I seen them earlier through the field glasses. Four of them there were."

"But there's no one there now," said Michael.

"No, sure it's nearly dark." He was not interested, but Michael remained staring out at the headland for quite some time.

* * *

Molly turned from the beam as it came again and leaned against the Boar's Tusk, pressing her forehead against its cold stone until the rage had drained out of her. "God forgive me," she sobbed, "Father, forgive me for I have sinned."

How could she ever again make her confession to old Father Conlon?

Suddenly she realized she was shivering. "I must get down out of here at once. No one must ever know I was up there." She plunged down the rocky track and twice she stumbled and fell. Distantly she heard Flossie bark, there was light in Uncle Peter's cottage, but Uncle Peter was happily frying the nice wee trout she had brought and did not open the door. The first big drops of the storm were falling and it would have been nice to shelter in the warmth of the cottage, but no! No one, not even Uncle Peter, must know she had not gone straight home after leaving him. She tried to hurry on the road, but found there was something wrong with her sandal. It had lost a heel. "Just as Michael said." She pushed the tricycle back onto the road, jumped on it and rattled off at a reckless speed down the hill and out along the straight flat road.

"Child, you're drownded," said her mother when she appeared dripping on the doorstep.

"I'll be all right when I'm home and changed." She tucked the plastic cover up under the boys' chins. "Thanks for keeping them," and she was gone.

* * *

As Henry entered the dining room, he was conscious that a hush had fallen on the room. He felt all eyes were on him, and not approvingly at that. Damn them. They could not expect him to go and look for her now in the dark and pouring rain. Sullenly he ate his meal without really noticing what was put before him. Silly woman. Why the hell couldn't she have come away with the rest of them. They had all begged her, he'd done his utmost. But no. Thrawn, that's what she was. He glared furiously at his coffee cup.

"No sign of the little lady?" It was the fisherman who had

spoken to him on their first night. "'Fraid she's going to be wet when she gets here."

"And not for the first time," growled Henry. "She's always doing daft things like this. But she's tough, she'll get here."

"But she might have sprained her ankle," twittered a bird-like little woman, "I mean, one doesn't like to think of her lying out in the rain, calling for help."

"Foolish to walk alone," said her husband, a tall, lean man who always walked with an alpenstock studded with badges. "Never less than three. One to stay with the casualty, one to go for help."

"Don't you think we ought to tell the Gardai?"

"Not much hope of them turning out on a night like this."

"If you drove the car, I would go with you," offered Mr Stafford. "and we could at least search the road."

"It must be very worrying for you," twittered the bird.

So Henry and Mr Stafford drove slowly along the empty road in the driving rain, carefully scanning the ditches on either hand. When they reached the top of the road, there was still a faint glimmer of light in Uncle Peter's cottage.

"I'll go up there and see, if they've seen or heard anything," said Mr Stafford, producing a large umbrella, "maybe they are sheltering her', he added brightly.

Flossie barked as the garden gate slammed behind him in the wind, and she continued barking ever more furiously as he mounted the path. Uncle Peter, candle in hand and in his nightshirt and carpet slippers, was about to get into bed, but peeped out to see who could be coming up his path at this hour of night, but saw nothing. He put on his long overcoat and took down his blackthorn off the rack. rummaging for the torch, when there came a knock on the door.

"Who is it?" he called. "What do you want?"

"I'm sorry to disturb you," a gentle, unmenacing voice said.

He opened the door and his candle blew out.

"For God's sake, come in, before the whole place is blown down." He flashed the torch over this miserable figure before him, whose umbrella had blown inside out.

"We're looking for a lady who was walking on the Boar's Snout and hasn't returned."

"I doubt you'll not find her this wild night. It's far too dangerous to go anywhere up on the edge."

"And you've heard nothing?"

"I'm sorry," he shook his head.

A very wet Mr Stafford returned to the car, and silently they drove away.

* * *

The guests had all drifted off to bed, finding the gloom unbearable, all but the little birdlike woman who had been twittering around trying to comfort everyone, and who had now elected to sit with Mrs Stafford until the men came back. At a glance they saw their errand had been fruitless.

"Thanks for coming," growled Henry, "like a whiskey?"

Mr Stafford was beginning to say that he did not drink, when his wife surprisingly said to the barman, "Make it a hot whiskey and put some lemon and sugar in it." She had observed with some annoyance that whereas her husband was drenched, Henry was relatively dry.

"Send a bottle up to my room," growled Henry and began to climb the stairs.

"Poor man," said the little bird, "it's the NOT KNOWING that's so awful," a remark she had made many times that evening.

But despite the whiskey, he could not sleep. He was stunned by the events of the day. Over and over again he went over so many "if only's". And now they would blame him. Yet he had done his best. It was all so unfair. In his own way he was fond of Marjorie, although there were some things he had never understood. That daft wild streak in her. He would miss her.

The bottle was nearly empty, when the lights of a car lit up his ceiling. It stopped now at the front door and after a few moments went away. He waited for the message that would surely come, but it was daylight before there was a quiet knock on his door. A fishing boat had picked up a body and the Gardai would like him to come and identify it at his convenience.

"I'm not sleeping. I might as well come now."

He was glad that none of the other residents was astir as he stumbled unsteadily down the stairs.

* * *

The Gardai had a busy morning, interviewing anybody who might have been on the Boar's Snout that evening. They went up to Uncle Peter's and sent two men out to the lighthouse, but to Michael's relief they only wanted to interview the officer who had been on duty. He did not know what he would have told them. Yes, he had seen the lady in the yellow anorak, standing on the edge waving, and he thought he had seen someone or something moving behind her, but he could not be sure. What kind of a statement was that? He could not be sure. As there was nothing to be seen, when next the beam came round, they would just think he wanted to make himself important.

And when next the boat came out with the supplies, the local paper had had a field day. "Death on Drumnahork" it screamed across three columns, and all the village saw its names in print, what each had said, where they had been and what they were doing at the time of the accident, all of which amounted to the fact that no one had seen anything and it was regrettably supposed the lady had slipped.

Dr Langenheim, the president of the Ramblers Club, contributed quite a piece on the Folly of People Walking Alone on Dangerous Places and of their companions for allowing them to do so.

At the very bottom of the page it stated that the Gardai had searched the whole area and tried to trace the deceased's last movements. Only beside the Boar's Tusk in the soft, peaty earth they found skid marks, in one of which the heel of a woman's shoe was plugged. Mrs Stafford stated that the deceased always wore sensible brogue shoes out walking, and no one paid any heed to that little paragraph except Michael.

For the last two weeks of his turn of duty he thought of nothing else. Every morning when he wakened, there it was – small, black, square, curvaceous on three sides and straight on the fourth. He remembered how it had felt in his pocket when they bought the sandals. He wondered if anyone had noticed them, if the salesman would remember him. He was glad he had not been wearing his white top. That woman had moved on, and anyway she was the only person who would not be able to speak now. He had been imagining things. He wanted desperately to ask Molly if she still had the sandals, if they had lost a heel, but no, he must not ask any daft questions over the telephone to the mainland. He must not be stupid. He wondered how Molly was feeling: had she read in the paper that the Gardai had found the heel of a woman's shoe on the Boar's Tusk? It might be the heel of anybody's shoe, mightn't it?

At last the day came and he could hardly stop himself from racing up from the harbour and into her arms. She also seemed overjoyed to see him and kept on almost tearfully kissing and clinging to him. Then they withdrew from each other and became almost like two strangers, making polite conversation about trivial matters in which neither of them were much interested. There was just one question he wanted to ask, and he could not bring himself to do it.

She looked pale, and for the first time he thought she looked frail. She confessed she had not been sleeping well and asked him to put some rat poison round the back. Rover had wakened her barking several times, and she had found it hard to go to sleep again. A reasonable excuse, but perhaps she had something on her mind? He felt she was watching him as he pottered idly about as if looking for something. Sometimes when he found her looking at him, she would drop her eyes at once and bend her head over whatever she was doing. She did not want to meet his eyes. There grew up a tension between them, each had withdrawn into themselves.

On the evening before his leave was up, he felt he could stand it no longer. Braving himself, he said casually, "I've not seen you wearing those new sandals we bought at the fair."

He saw a flicker of fear flash in her eyes as she turned away. But she recovered herself in a moment. "Ugh, those things! They were never meant for the wet of this place. The heel came off, just like you said it would, and I threw them away."

"Where?"

Again the flash of fear.

"On the rubbish heap. Can't rightly remember."

It was the first time she had lied to him, and Molly was not a good liar.

"No, I mean where did it come off?"

Again the glint of fear.

"Och, somewhere out along the road." She hung her head over her sewing.

He bent down. "On the Boar's Snout?" he whispered.

"Oh, Michael, you've guessed," she sobbed. "I've wanted so much to talk, to explain – to you or anybody."

"Well, I hope to hell you didn't."

She shook her head. "You've no idea what it's been like these last weeks keeping everything bottled up."

"Oh yes, I know. Listen, Molly," he put a hand firmly on each of her shoulders, "you and I are the only people who know what happened that night up on the Boar's Snout, and that's the way it's going to stay. No one will ever know. I don't want to hear what came over you or how it happened, it's over and done with now. So we will never mention it again, not even between ourselves."

Her hysterical sobbing grew less, and when at last it ceased, she whispered, "Michael, after what I've done, can you ever love me again?"

"More than ever, my own wee goose."

STAMP DUTY

Miss Corscadden did not like the new Christmas stamps. For nearly thirty years she had been postmistress in Carrickreagh, and innovations upset her. Blindfold she could have broken off any given number of stamps from a sheet, but these new stamps were a different shape and she lost her bearings. She felt they had just been designed to make her look foolish.

"Them's nice, aren't they?" said Flo, leaning towards her. Flo had a habit of leaning her elbows on the counter so that her ample young bosom bulged over her plump arms. Miss Corscadden had spoken to her about it, even suggesting the slimming effects of an overall, but Flo was a simple, easy-going soul, and many things which worried her aunt did not bother her at all.

"Gaudy," said Miss Corscadden. "Gold, even down to the margin."

But Flo had resumed interest in "What the Stars Foretell".

"Here, girl, straighten the place up. I think I hear the bus coming," said her aunt sharply. "I've told you before about reading the customers' papers."

"It's only Maggie's, and she won't mind," said Flo. She slapped the pile together without making it look much tidier.

Two schoolboys tumbled off the bus and into the shop, followed shortly by Mr McCutcheon. the schoolmaster.

"Please, can you give us six stamps for Christmas cards," said Willy Gillespie, "the new ones, I mean."

"My Ma says they'd had no call to put our good Queen's head on them Papish pictures," said Willy's friend.

"My Da says it was just the right place to put it," said Willy.

Miss Corscadden said nothing. The dignity of the postmistress demanded an impartial reticence in such matters.

"Good afternoon," said Mr McCutcheon. He gave the crown of his greasy Homburg a little squeeze by way of greeting the ladies. "I want one each of the new stamps, please. It's for my friend in Luxembourg, the one who collects the new issues."

"Hey, missis," said Willy suddenly, "there's no wee heads on my stamps at all." He thrust them under the grill.

True enough, there were not.

"Yon's the queer thing," said Miss Corscadden, slipping for once off her pedestal as postmistress and falling into the local idiom.

The machine which did the gold overprinting seemed to have hopped to the left, leaving the row of stamps at the right of the sheet unprinted and, instead, printing the Queen's head in the left-hand margin, as Miss Corscadden had noticed.

Mr McCutcheon's face was pressed close to the grill. His little eyes gleamed bright and round behind his spectacles.

"I'll buy Willy's stamps," he said, stretching his thin fingers under the grill, "I don't mind."

"I'm sorry," said Miss Corscadden, laying her chilblained ones on the stamps, "I can't sell them if they're misprinted."

"My friend in Luxembourg would be delighted to add a misprint to his collection, just as a curiosity."

"I'm sorry, but those are my regulations."

"If you were to sell the whole row, who would know?" Mr McCutcheon smiled winningly, revealing an absent tooth.

"Here, Willy, there's six good ones for you," said Miss Corscadden.

As the boys left, Mr McCutcheon dropped his voice and said, "I'd pay you more than their face value."

"Mr McCutcheon, it's no good. I know my duty. There's the stamps you asked for."

Sadly Mr McCutcheon gave his hat a final squeeze as he shuffled out of the door.

Miss Corscadden put the "beheaded' stamps into an envelope, sealed it up and popped it into her desk.

"Och, Auntie, why wouldn't you let him have one?" asked Flo. "Sure, it's of no value anyway."

"No value, my foot," snapped Miss Corscadden, "there's some people daft enough to pay any amount of money for misprints. And Andy McCutcheon knows that as well as I do," she added.

"Well, fancy," said Flo. She reflected for a moment, which was about as long as Flo ever reflected about anything. "Seems daft. Dear help him, he's probably lonely since his wife died," and, leaning on the counter in her usual manner, Flo began to flip over the pages of the children's comics.

* * *

Later that evening Miss Corscadden found Mr McCutcheon seated with Flo in the back parlour.

"I called round to see if we could have a little chat," he said.

"Is it the stamps again?" asked Miss Corscadden.

"Well – eh – yes."

"I'm sending them back to Newtownards."

"Miss Corscadden, I know you to be a woman of great integrity, a pillar of the church here in Carrickreagh. I would never wish you to do anything against your conscience, but, after all, conscience should only rule between right and wrong. In this case you would not be wronging anyone. It's not like stealing the stamps, just selling them without noticing that they were misprints – like, in fact, you did to young Willy." Gleaning encouragement from her silence, he went on, "Now – if you could just bring yourself to make the same mistake again – that's all I'm asking you to do – a simple mistake that no one could blame you for – I would sell the stamps, say in London, and we could maybe share the proceeds, if you see what I mean."

"Think of that, Auntie, you could be rich."

"If you'll just let me manage your affairs, we could all be rich," said Mr McCutcheon, smiling at Flo. Flo gave one of her gleeful squawks and all but nudged the schoolmaster in the ribs.

"We've all admired the way you've reared poor Flo here. No one could have done more for her, not even her own parents, had they been spared. But it can't always have been easy for you." That was true, certainly. "I dare say you haven't been able to put past as much as you would have wished for your retirement." True, too. "Well, here's your opportunity. You've served the Post Office loyally and well for as long as I can remember, and now the Post Office has made it possible for you to reap a little well-deserved reward without harming anyone. You owe it to yourself."

Miss Corscadden was beginning to feel that the clear-cut outlines of her precise world were growing blurred and hazy. "Indeed, I don't know what to think," she sighed.

"Just think of all the holidays we could have, the grand places we could go to," said Flo.

"Well, anyhow, before you throw away this wonderful opportunity, please, I beg of you, think over what I've been saying," said Mr McCutcheon. rising to go. "But not a word of this to anyone, ladies. We'll keep this little secret to ourselves," and, revealing his gap tooth, he imparted to Flo, at any rate, a pleasurable feeling of conspiracy.

* * *

During the days which followed, Miss Corscadden frequently thought over what Mr McCutcheon had said. It kept on coming between her and her work. She found it hard to concentrate, she became flustered when counting out the new stamps, once she gave wrong change, which was very unusual for her. It upset her very much. And every time she opened her drawer she saw the envelope lying there. She could have given it to the postman, but she felt uneasy at letting it out of her hands. She wanted to deliver it in person to the manager in Newtownards. But that meant it would have to lie there until her next half-day, next Thursday.

Flo, by contrast, was more than usually lively. Slamming around the kitchen, she sometimes was ready to sweep out the shop before Miss Corscadden had unlocked it, and had to ask for the keys. Miss Corscadden always came and unlocked it for her, because on that keyring was also the key of her desk.

As Christmas drew nearer, business in the little shop grew brisker. Flo enjoyed helping customers choose presents, fill stockings or select Christmas cards, tittering together as they read out the verses inside. Miss Corscadden hoped she was not making too many mistakes with the prices. She herself was too busy at the Post Office end to keep a proper eye on Flo, in fact, there were days when she was almost walled in with brown paper parcels. And every day after school Mr McCutcheon came in to buy some little thing. He did not mention the stamps again, but lingered down at Flo's end of the counter, talking to her. There were now so many people in the shop, Miss Corscadden could not always hear what they were saying, but Flo seemed to giggle a great deal, and one day as Flo was leaning over the counter in her usual blousy way, her great moon face smiling into his, a startling idea came into Miss Corscadden's head. At that moment Flo let off one of her more raucous guffaws, and Miss Corscadden dismissed the idea. In any case, Mr McCutcheon was old enough to be the girl's father.

Thursday came and went. Miss Corscadden felt too tired to face a crowded bus journey. She would go into Newtownards some time after Christmas when things were easier. So the envelope still lay in her desk.

* * *

The Carol Service had been arranged for the Wednesday before Christmas. Flo appeared wearing on her head a monstrous concoction of pink net, liberally studded with sequins and pearl drops.

"Child dear, you're not going to the church in that?" asked her startled aunt.

"Och, Auntie, you're just not 'with it' these days. Maggie said it was fit for a honeymoon," and Flo gave one of her shrieks.

There was no time to argue, so they set out, Miss Corscadden reflecting that anyway it would be dark, at least on the way to church.

A few branches of straggling holly had done little to induce the festive spirit into Carrickreagh Presbyterian Church, nor had the not-long-lit heating done much for its sepulchral chill. The keys of the harmonium felt cold and stiff under Miss Corscadden's chilblained fingers. Flo's spirits, however, were quite undaunted. There was no need to harken to her as a herald angel for, as was afterwards agreed, you could have heard her at the crossroads. The sequins and the pearl drops shivered and shook.

Then, like cattle when a strange dog enters the field, the congregation raised their heads and turned to stare. Out of the corner of her eye Miss Corscadden was aware of Mr McCutcheon coming up the aisle. Such a thing had never happened before. The singing faltered. She herself, who never faltered, not even that day when the plaster fell, slithered over several wrong notes. Flo alone forged ahead like a Lambeg drum.

With relief Miss Corscadden fumbled on to the final "Amen" and slipped out, wishing the Minister a perfunctory Happy Christmas. Flo was waiting for her, the porch light falling full on that terrible hat.

"That was most enjoyable," said Mr McCutcheon, stepping out of the shadow, "most enjoyable."

Miss Corscadden threw him a quick look to see if he were "having her on", but only caught the noncommittal glint of his spectacles in the dark. They all walked down the road together, Flo bidding "Happy Christmas" to all and sundry.

"I think we ought to ask Mr McCutcheon in, Auntie," she said. "I'm sure he could do with a cuppa to warm up after that place."

Miss Corscadden assented, but without relish. She felt a headache coming on.

"That would indeed be kind," said Mr McCutcheon.

"Flo, bring me an aspirin, please, when you come," whispered Miss Corscadden. She hastened to poke up the parlour fire, whilst Flo went into the kitchen.

"It's a delight to find a young person enjoying her singing like Flo does," said Mr McCutcheon, settling down in the best chair. "She certainly was in great voice tonight."

Again Miss Corscadden threw him a look, but again was met by the blank reflection of the firelight on his spectacles.

"Have you thought any more of my little proposition?" he asked, leaning forward smiling. His gap tooth was showing and he looked like a knowing alligator.

"Indeed, I have," said Miss Corscadden.

"And to what conclusion have you come?"

"I've decided to do nothing until we've got Christmas over," she said. "I just don't seem to get time to think these days."

"Yes, of course. Where matters of principle are concerned, it doesn't do to be hasty."

Flo blundered in with the tea tray.

"I couldn't find the aspirins, Auntie," she said. "Give us your keys and I'll get you some out of the shop.

"You can't have looked properly, child."

"Honest, Auntie, I looked everywhere. Och, come on, give us your keys and lets have some tea. I'm dying for a cup."

Miss Corscadden hesitated. She did not wish to disclose in front of Mr McCutcheon that she never gave Flo the keys. She was aware that his spectacles were focused on her like spotlights.

"Well, mind you lock up properly afterwards," she said and handed them over.

"Have you ever thought of having Flo's voice trained?" asked Mr McCutcheon with sudden enthusiasm. "I always think it's such a pity that young people born in a place like Carrickreagh have no opportunity to develop their talents. Oh yes, there's the expenses. But there again, if you'd just agree to my little proposition, we could soon afford Flo a few singing lessons. All she needs is just a bit of training with a good teacher. Sure, look at our Jimmy. If James Galway hadn't had a good teacher, he'd still be tootling his flute up and down the Shankill Road with some Orange band or other, and look at him now. Tootling in all the capitals of the world, a villa in Switzerland and several marriages. You could be giving Flo her big chance." Flo returned with the aspirins, and then Miss Corscadden could have sworn – not that Miss Corscadden ever did – she gave McCutcheon a wink.

Mr McCutcheon prattled on. Flo seemed to find him entertaining, but her aunt entirely lost the trend of the conversation. Her head ached and her chilblains itched with the warmth of the room. She wished he would go.

At last Flo showed him out, taking her time to do so, and tired though she was, Miss Corscadden at once sprang up and unlocked the shop and her desk. To her relief the envelope still lay there, but yet apprehension returned when, as Mr McCutcheon passed the window, she thought she saw him rubbing his hands together as if in extreme satisfaction.

Miss Corscadden had a bad night. Her sleep was invaded by a shimmering pink blancmange, studded all over with little gold heads which winked and twinkled like spectacles, and a wily alligator sidling down the garden path, pursued by the Minister's booming echo, "Upon thy belly shalt thou go."

That decided her. She would get rid of the stamps before she went dotty and, as it was Thursday, she would do it that afternoon.

The manager of the Post Office had known Miss Corscadden for many years. "And what can I do for you?" he asked as he showed her to a seat in his office. She told him, and as she laid the envelope on his desk she felt like a faithful retriever dog.

"You certainly did right to bring them here yourself," he said, slitting open the envelope. She enjoyed being patted. "But," said the manager, "there's nothing wrong with these stamps."

She stared. There was not.

"But I'm sure, I know I put them in there. There were no little heads on them then. All the heads were down the margin." The manager was studying her gravely. "I'm sure you think I must be going dotty," she said lamely.

"Not at all, Miss Corscadden. But I do think that perhaps you could do with a break. I know what the Christmas rush is like nowadays. And, let's face it, we're none of us getting any younger." He was a kindly man, enquiring about eyesight, headaches and sleep at night, but for all that Miss Corscadden did not feel inclined to tell him about the pink blancmange or the alligator.

"We'll try and find you a substitute as soon as we can," he continued, "but for that you'll have to be seen by a doctor. Now there's a very good man up at the hospital here, one of these new psychiatrists, I'll give you his name and you must make an appointment. You can either see him here or in Downpatrick."

She stared at the card he offered. Then in a numb voice she said "Downpatrick? That's up in the Asylum, isn't it?"

"Miss Corscadden, dear. It's not that nowadays. No, no, you mustn't think of it like that. They deal with nervous complaints, overstrain and such. You don't have to be mental to go there. No, no, you can put that idea right out of your bead."

Miss Corscadden did not entirely, but she put the card in her handbag. Miserably she left the office.

The first drops of rain were beginning to fall. Dazed and bewildered she walked towards the buses, hardly noticing where she went. She had made a complete fool of herself. The manager had been very understanding, had tried to make it look like some sort of bilious attack, but there was no dodging the fact that he thought her sufficiently deranged to go and see someone in what to Miss Corscadden would always be "The Asylum". She almost passed Mr McCutcheon without seeing him. She looked back, but he hurried on as if he had not seen her. She was sure it was Mr McCutcheon, at least as sure as she could be about anything anymore. She watched him hurry across the street, carrying a heavy suitcase, his head down hunched against the rain, his hat shielding his face. But that was Mr McCutcheon's hat. She might be going dotty, but she would know that misshapen old hat anywhere. Yet the figure got into the bus for Belfast and, settling in the back seat, disappeared behind a newspaper. Miss Corscadden climbed into the Carrickreagh bus.

Ought she really to see them at the Mental Hospital? She watched the raindrops wriggling like tadpoles across the windows of the bus. Certainly, she had not been herself lately, and she felt people were beginning to notice. It all seemed to have started the day they brought out those new stamps.

The bus slowed down to absorb a gaggle of schoolboys,

and she saw Willy Gillespie amongst them. That was an idea; if he remembered the misprints, that would prove she was not imagining seeing gold heads before her eyes. But she had already made a big enough fool of herself that day and she shrank into her corner.

Willy spotted her. "I say, Missis," he said, "have you any more of them stamps? The wrong 'uns, I mean." She shook her head. "My Da says you get a lot of money for them if you know where to sell them. Pounds and pounds, he says. Daft, giving pounds for a wee bit of sticky paper that costs a few pence, and it not printed right either."

She gave the boy one of her rare but very sweet smiles. She was beginning to recover. She had corroboration.

There was light in Flo's bedroom when she got home.

'You can't come in, Auntie," she said. "I – I'm packing my Christmas presents." She sounded flushed and flustered.

Miss Corscadden went into the parlour. The fire was nearly out, and there was no sign of tea. That was the trouble with Flo. She never could keep more than one idea in her head at a time. Miss Corscadden sank into a chair. Suddenly she was alerted by the click of a suitcase being shut, and in that instant things clicked into place in Miss Corscadden's head. Flo was not packing Christmas presents.

Miss Corscadden went up the narrow staircase. "And where do you think you're off to?" she asked.

"Auntie, you gave me a turn." The pink hat was perched ready for flight on the corner of the mirror.

"I suppose you think Andy McCutcheon's waiting for you at the garden gate?"

"Please, Auntie, don't be angry with us."

"Let me tell you, he's left for Belfast this afternoon."

"He's never," said Flo aghast.

"He's probably in London by now, or maybe Paris, dear knows."

"But he said he'd take me to Paris."

"And you believed him, you poor silly girl." Flo began to cry. "It was you that changed the envelopes in my desk last night, wasn't it?"

"Och, Auntie, I meant no harm. And Andy said it wasn't like stealing. It wasn't harming anyone, he said. Honest." She fondled the hat. "Just the thing for Paris, he said."

"Once he got the stamps out of you, that was the end of that, I'm afraid."

"Och, Auntie, he's never gone, he's never. I don't believe it, Auntie. He's not away without me. It's not true, not true." Poor Flo flung herself sobbing onto the bed. The hat bounced onto the floor and rolled unheaded, Miss Corscadden decided it was best to let Flo cry herself out, and went downstairs.

She stood for a few moments before the parlour fire, considering what she should do. A psychiatrist would have little difficulty in proving that Flo was of low intelligence, easily influenced by others, and possibly not even entirely responsible for her actions. He could persuade the authorities to be more lenient with her than with Mr McCutcheon.

Miss Corscadden was quite her old self when she entered the shop. With a clear head and a firm step she went across to the phone and, taking the manager's card from her handbag, she made an appointment for Flo. Then she rang the police and cited Mr McCutcheon as a receiver of stolen goods. Then she went upstairs with a cup of tea for Flo.

COMMOTION IN GOZO

The heavy, dolphin-knockered door of the *Duke of Edinburgh* stood ajar, and I was able to slip out without rousing the hotel staff. That they were already up and about, I knew, for I had heard Therese's voice for more than an hour directing the young girls in the yard, in fact that, coupled with the incessant church bells, was the reason why at six in the morning I had decided that I might better employ my time than by trying to sleep.

Outside a surprising number of people were abroad, mostly workmen, climbing into lorries or starting off on bicycles to begin their day's work, I stepped out gaily. I, too, in a way, was going to work. With a box of paints and a canvas borrowed from my host of the night before, I was about to spend an hour or so in the cool of the morning painting in the market square. Or at least that was my intention.

The first difficulty was that my loan included neither easel nor stool. I made enquiring gestures about the ownership of an empty packing case and placed my paraphernalia on it. Nearby was an orange box doing nothing, so I collected that and sat down on it. Hardly had I settled myself when the proprietor of the café across the way presented me with a chair.

"Is better," he said, smiling and bowing.

I smiled, bowed, thanked him and resettled myself.

Grimly I began to squash colours out of the reluctant tubes. It was then that I began to feel a little self-conscious sitting by myself in the middle of the market square. I felt that after such kind attention, something would be expected of me. I remembered a similar feeling, when once, as a member of Miss Nairn's dancing class, we tots had entered the Ulster Hall to demonstrate to our mamas and the assembled company how we washed our clothes. It was while we were showing them how we hung up our clothes that my eye caught sight of the paintings high up on the walls, some of which I knew to have been done by our friend and neighbour Mr Carey, and it was only the tittering applause which brought me back to earth, to the agonized beckonings of my mother and the realization that my classmates had long since finished their make-believe laundry and departed, leaving me a sole performer in that vast place, with the audience beginning to expect more of me than just star-gazing. So now, too, a similar sense of inadequacy settled on me. It was years since I put brush to canvas, in fact, I am really only a holiday sketcher nowadays, but I could not very well make a proclamation to that effect in the market place. I realized that a preliminary try-out in private might have been more prudent.

My subject was a fairly simple one – or at least it was when I started. A market stall in the shade of the trees, tended by a buxom lady in a red jumper with a sunlit façade in the background. Not too many people.

Occasionally people strolled by and had a look to see how I was getting on, but on the whole they did not come too close nor stay too long. The whole thing, I told myself, was to pay no heed and to concentrate. There always comes a time in all paintings when you wish you had never begun, when the temptation to complete some little corner in detail rather than plod on and cover the whole of the canvas becomes very strong. You want to pander to the audience by producing something recognizable. Deaf and blind to all around except the scene in front, I splurged doggedly on.

My solitude was presently penetrated by a voluble little man with a wrinkled monkey's face. His remarks were apparently addressed to me. He wanted something. Under his white cap his twinkly little eyes implored me earnestly. He drew nearer and laid his hands on the packing case. I indicated that, of course, he could have it, but at once we were the centre of an angry crowd. They were all on my side, and everybody seemed to have a great deal to say to the stall-holder.

"Please, for you, Miss," said a cheerful youth, offering a very rickety tomato box.

Whether the "Miss" was due to faulty English or to politeness, or to the fact that no matron of Gozo, or indeed anywhere else, had ever been known to give a pre-breakfast performance like this in a public square will never be known. The crowd was suddenly scattered by the café proprietor, who, with a tremendously gallant gesture presented me with a second chair.

"I make you plenty room," he said, and with further vigorous flourishes did so.

But despite his efforts, once having collected a crowd I never quite lost it again. More stalls were being set up and many more people were filling the square. Shyly at first, the children edged closer. Whiffs of vanilla were wafted around me from the bulging shopping bags. A blessing that they do not seem to eat much garlic in Gozo. A portly lady, enveloped in a voluminous *faldetta* and an all-pervading smell of celery, hovered above me like the Angel of Death. For several minutes the black canvas slippers of the parish priest were stationed beside me. I could hear his beads clicking as he breathed. He had a rounded prow, and the beads rocked gently to and fro like the painter of an idle dinghy.

By now the sun was hot on the back of my neck and the glare was beginning to get troublesome. My painting was not going well, but I doubted if dark glasses would help it. What it needed was a tea break, a stretching of the legs and a long cool look. But how to convey this to my circle of onlookers – I would not dare call them admirers? They, poor dears, were still hoping for a pretty picture. I felt like an incompetent shot surrounded by eager, panting gun-dogs. Heads swivelled Wimbledon-wise following my brush from palette to canvas.

"Aha, basket," said an approving voice, relaying the landfall of the yellow ochre to his fellows.

A peculiar beastie lit on the canvas. To the titters of the children I shepherded it off with the palette knife. Another one arrived, but I pretended not to notice, as I was still painting out the tracks of the first. Little sunburned fingers crept over my shoulder to point to its position and, as I still took no notice, to poke it towards the edge of the canvas. My work was beginning to show distinct traces of the Abstract influence, Collage in fact, as one of the beasties had left its wing behind. I began to paint in starts distractedly, daubing hither and thither, as much attempting to smother the peculiarities as to depict the scene before me. Therese's greeting of the previous evening echoed through my head. "You like a cup of tea, please? OK I bring. Is all right, all right. I bring. No trouble." Bless her heart. Meaning no disrespect to His Royal Highness, Therese IS the *Duke of Edinburgh*.

Looking up, I found that somehow I seemed to have become the centre of a religious procession. Like the transformation scene in the pantomime, the square had become flooded with charming little choirboys in frilly surplices and birettas, all beaming at me and craning their necks to see my picture as they passed. All around people were acknowledging their passing, and I felt that some such recognition was expected from me, too, but as I held two long brushes across my mouth like cats' whiskers I felt the gesture would be inappropriate. Maybe that was what gave the choir the giggles, I don't know. More than ever I felt in need of a nice cup of tea.

As the children closed around me once more, I knew that I

was losing my grip. For one thing, my original subject was completely obliterated by a mass of people, mostly in black, and black is not a rewarding colour to paint. Like the broomsticks in the *Sorcerer's Apprentice*, more and more black figures with sunburned faces swirled and eddied round the stalls. Whenever I substituted a blouse or shirt from my imagination, a ripple of astonishment went through my audience. My models were all known, probably related, to them, and they wished to see their relations recorded true to life. Aunt Anastasia was obviously a respected matron, who would never let herself be seen in the market place in a lemon-coloured blouse like any brazen tourist. I looked to see if my borrowed box contained any black. It did, but its owner did not seem to use it any more than I did, and I could not get the cap off. Well, if I could not get the cap off the black paint, Aunt Anastasia would just have to shame posterity in a lemon-coloured blouse. Unaware of her fate, she had, in any case, wandered further on in search of fish.

Subversion in the scent of sizzling bacon seeped into my consciousness. By now the others would be sitting down to breakfast, and the *Duke of Edinburgh*, disregarding both the thermometer and the Malta Labour Party, serves an uncompromisingly British breakfast, in which the crisp, crusty local bread fries to a golden perfection. The time had come to make an end.

Spellbound, the children watched me scrape the colours off the palette, wipe the knife on a piece of paper, indicate (ineffectively) that what I now wanted was a litter basket, and finally place the paper under one of the chairs, where I felt it would soon be swooped on as a squishy souvenir. I rose and bowed my gratitude to the distant café proprietor, hoping that he would collect his chairs before anyone else did, and gathering together my paintbox, sticky canvas and the last shreds of my dignity, I quit the stage, trying to keep ahead of the children without actually running.

Something objectionable had attached itself to my right sandal and was squelching between my toes. It was I who had collected the squishy souvenir.

"You lost it, yes?" said the taxi-driver.

Desperately trying to disengage my right foot, I ignored the man.

"Please," he repeated, "you lost it," and with a courtly grace proffered my glasses.